Miss Spider's Tea Party

paintings and verse by David Kirk

Scholastic Inc.
Callaway

New York Toronto London Auckland Sydney Mexico City New Delhi Hong Kong

ONE lonely spider sipped her tea
While gazing at the sky.
She watched the insects on the leaves
And many flying by.
"If I had friends like these," she sighed,
"Who'd stay a while with me,
I'd sit them down on silken chairs
And serve them cakes and tea."

Two timid beetles — Ike and May —
Crept from the woodwork that same day.
But when Miss Spider begged, "Please stay?"
They shrieked, "Oh no!" and dashed away.

Three fireflies flew inside that night,
Their spirits high, their tails alight.
They spied the web and squeaked in fear,
"We'd better get away from here!"
The little trio did not feel
They'd care to be a spider's meal.

Four bumblebees buzzed by outside.
"Please come to tea!" Miss Spider cried.
The four ignored her swaying there.
She waved a tea towel in the air.
She took a cup and tapped the glass.
Then one bee spoke to her at last:
"We would be fools to take our tea
With anyone so spidery."

Within the shadows of the room,
Just peeking from behind a broom,
Five grinning faces bobbed and peered.
Miss Spider smiled. Her heart was cheered.
Descending for a closer look,
She danced into the gloomy nook
But sadly found those jolly mugs
Belonged, alas! to rubber bugs.

Some ants strode in, they numbered six,
But ants with spiders will not mix.
She brewed them tea from hips of roses;
The proud platoon turned up their noses.

A fine bouquet concealed its prize
Of seven dainty butterflies.
Miss Spider, watching from the wall,
Was not aware of them at all.

The tea table was set for eight
With saucers, cups, and silver plate.
The cakes were fresh, the service gleamed,
Yet no one would arrive, it seemed.
Her company in no demand
Left her a cup for every hand.

Nine spotted moths kept safe and warm
In shelter from a thunderstorm.
They stood beneath an open sash
And watched the jagged lightning flash.
Miss Spider dropped down on a thread,
A silver tray above her head.
She'd hoped to please them, but instead . . .